Chr imas

*T*he Fairy Bell Sisters all
love Christmas.
And this year it looks like
they will be welcoming a
very special visitor for the
festivities...

Other *Fairy Bell Sisters* stories:

The Fairy Bell Sisters

Winter Magic

First published in Great Britain in paperback by
HarperCollins *Children's Books* in 2014
HarperCollins *Children's Books* is a division of HarperCollins*Publishers* Ltd,
77-85 Fulham Palace Road, Hammersmith, London, W6 8JB.

The HarperCollins website address is: www.harpercollins.co.uk

1

Text copyright © Margaret McNamara 2014
Illustrations copyright © Erica-Jane Waters 2014

ISBN 978-0-00-752326-9

Margaret McNamara and Erica-Jane Waters assert the moral right to be
identified as the author and illustrator of the work.

Printed and bound in England by Clays Ltd, St Ives plc

MIX
Paper from
responsible sources
FSC
www.fsc.org
FSC™ C007454

FSC™ is a non-profit international organisation established to promote
the responsible management of the world's forests. Products carrying the
FSC label are independently certified to assure consumers that they come
from forests that are managed to meet the social, economic and
ecological needs of present and future generations,
and other controlled sources.

Find out more about HarperCollins and the environment at
www.harpercollins.co.uk/green

For Becky,
who loves Christmas

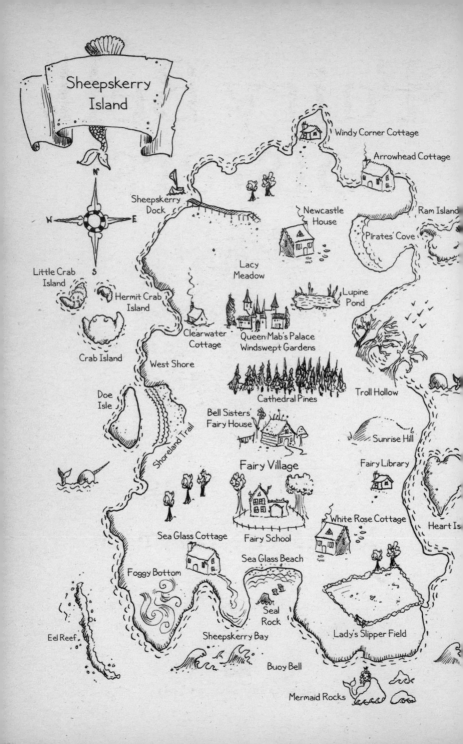

The Fairy Bell Sisters

Winter Magic

Margaret McNamara

Illustrations by Erica-Jane Waters

HarperCollins *Children's Books*

Chapter One

"This Christmas will be the perfect Christmas," said Lily Bell one sparkling December morning. "I'll have so many presents!"

The Fairy Bell sisters were lying on the hearth rug before a roaring fire in the great room of their fairy house. It was a blindingly sun-filled morning with fresh snow sparkling on every rooftop of the fairy village.

"Only ten more days until Christmas," said Silver Bell. She was stroking a tiny kitten that was curled up in the crook of her arm. "We don't know if we can wait any longer than that, do we, Ginger?" she said. Ginger purred.

"Well, you won't have to," said Clara. "Christmas is coming whether we'll be ready or not."

"I'm ready now," said Lily.

"We'll be patient, won't we, Squeakie?" said Rosie Bell. She rubbed Squeak's tummy.

"*O-bee!*" said Squeak.

"Why not, Squeak? Why won't you be patient?" said Rosie. Squeak rolled over and rubbed her back on the side of her cot. "I don't know what's the matter with Squeak. She hasn't been at all herself lately."

"Maybe she's getting a new tooth," said Silver.

"Or she has an upset tummy," said Clara. "Lily, have you been giving Squeak fairy chocolates again?"

"Not too many," said Lily.

"I'm a little worried about her," said Rosie. "Do you think—"

Just then there was a tinkling of bells outside their fairy house windows. "What's that?" asked Clara. The bells had a tone that she recognised from long ago, but she did not want to risk saying what she thought. She flew over to open the door – and found no one there.

"Try the back door," said Lily. "Maybe it's Avery. She said she'd come and visit later on today."

The tinkling sound came again. Rosie looked at Clara. *Could it be?*

Silver flew to the back door and opened it. "No one here, either," she said.

Once more the bell tinkled. Ginger

scurried into the kitchen to hide.

"Look! There at the window!" cried Rosie.

A dazzling beam of light filled the largest window of the fairy house great room.

"*Squeak!*" said Squeak.

The light was so bright and powerful that it seemed to be knocking right on the windowpane.

Clara took Rosie's hand and squeezed it tight. "She's come back, Rosie," whispered Clara. "She's come back at last."

 Chapter Two

It would be terribly rude to go much further in this story without introducing all of you to the Fairy Bell sisters. If you haven't had the pleasure of meeting them already, please do so now. Here are:

Clara Bell

Lily Bell

Silver Bell

Rosie Bell

Squeak

Clara, Rosie, Lily, Silver and Squeak
live together with the other young fairies
on Sheepskerry Island, which is a place
so filled with magic that you might be
reading this story very near it right now

(only you might not know it because human people call it by another name). The Fairy Bell sisters have one more member of their family, their big sister, who lives in Neverland with a friend called Peter Pan. In case you don't dare guess her name, I'll tell you: it's Tinker Bell. And it was Tinker Bell who had made that tinkling sound right outside the Fairy Bell sisters' fairy house.

If you have read other stories about the Fairy Bell sisters, you know that now is the time I usually ask a question to see if you *really* want to read any further. The question could be about perfect fairies or foolish fairies or headstrong fairies or fairies with tender hearts.

In times past, most of you have turned the pages and read on, which is why you know so much about the Fairy Bell sisters. But this time, I'm going to take a chance. I'm *not* going to ask that question, because I believe that every single one of you will want to read a story about a magical little baby who's about to make a big change. A little baby who has a secret language all her own. A little baby named Euphemia Bell, better known as Squeak.

You might especially want to read this story if I add that it is absolutely filled with magic and it's about a Christmas that almost does not happen – a Christmas that is an absolute disaster…

until Squeakie Bell discovers the most extraordinary Christmas present in all of Fairyland.

So get yourself cosy and wrap up warm if it's cold outside. And then let's see if you do go ahead and turn that page...

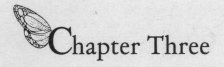Chapter Three

Oh, I just knew you would! You won't be sorry!

Chapter Four

"What is all this?" said Rosie.

"Did Christmas come early?"asked
Silver.

Clara pushed open the window
against the snow. The beam of light
grew brighter and the bell sound was
even higher and more clear. The great
room was bathed in a brilliant light,
which dissolved into tiny crystals. The
crystals gathered in front of the roaring

fire. They didn't melt like snowflakes. Instead, they swirled together into words.

"What is it?" asked Silver. She had never seen such a thing before in her life.

But Lily had. She remembered a message like this on her ninth birthday, a very special message indeed. "It's from Tinker Bell!" she cried.

The moment Lily Bell said the words 'Tinker Bell' the crystals swirled into shapes. And the shapes turned into words. And the words chimed. From Tinker Bell, they said.

"Tink!" cried Clara. "Is that really you?"

Of course it's me, chimed the words. **Only Tinker Bell can do things like this!**

"It's not Tink herself," Rosie whispered. "But it's Tink's magic!"

"Let's listen to what she's saying," said Lily. "Quick! Before the crystals disappear!"

The words sparkled and glowed as they chimed aloud.

Christmas is only ten days away, they said. **I know you are working hard to make it the best Christmas ever...**

"We are!" cried Silver.

But now I want you to stop working and not do another thing. Because I will do everything for you this Christmas.

"Does that mean you'll come home, Tink?" asked Silver.

"Hush, Silver," said Clara. "It's magic."

The words continued to appear.

I want to treat you to the very best Christmas you could ever have, they chimed. I'll bring every single present from Neverland and a tree too – with special decorations from Peter and the Lost Boys.

"*Aahma*!" said Squeak.

Mind you don't lift a finger. Leave it all to me. I'm in charge this year. See you early on the morning of the twenty-fourth of December, if not before! Love, Tink.

The Fairy Bell sisters watched the words Love, Tink until they faded from sight.

Silver was the first to speak. "Do you really think—"

But her words were interrupted by another flash.

P.S. I will be very cross if you spoil my surprise by decorating for Christmas and making presents for each other, so PLEASE DO NOT. That means you too, Rosie. xoxo T

Just to be on the safe side, the sisters didn't speak for quite a long time.

"Do you think she means it?" asked Clara at last. Clara knew from experience that sometimes Tinker Bell had trouble keeping her promises.

"Oh, she'll come! She'll come for sure. And she'll bring Christmas with her!" said Silver. Silver had been so young when Tink left for Neverland that she barely remembered her oldest sister. Sometimes she even forgot what Tink looked like. "I want to see her so much."

"Squeakie, aren't you happy?" asked Rosie.

But Squeakie, usually the cheeriest baby on Sheepskerry Island (or anywhere else), only gave a tiny smile.

"Squeakie's too young to know much about Christmas," said Lily, giving her baby sister a cuddle. "But, oh my! I can only imagine what Tink will bring me from Neverland. She knows I have wonderful taste!"

Silver was so thrilled that she flew around the great room in circles at the thought of Tinker Bell being here on Sheepskerry Island. "Now I really can't wait until Christmas," said Silver. "It's going to be the best Christmas of my entire life!"

 Chapter Five

There's nowhere quite as beautiful as Sheepskerry Island after a snowfall. The land is silent. The trees are laden down with heavy white powder that sparkles with tiny crystals of colour. Fairies have wings, of course, but they all love to make the first tracks in new-fallen snow. And that's exactly what the Fairy Bell sisters were doing one week before Christmas.

"The snow's stopped. Can we go outside, Clara?" asked Silver.

"If you wrap up warmly, including a hat, Lily," said Clara.

"I finally found a hat that makes me look adorable *and* keeps me warm," said Lily. "Thank goodness."

"Let's go and make snow fairies. Oh, but not you, Ginger," said Silver. "The snow is too deep for a kitten. You stay here where it's warm."

Ginger scampered over to the hearth rug and licked her fur by the fire.

"Mind you put your wings carefully on the wing table before you go out in the snow," said Clara. "I don't want them to get wet. You know it's not good

30

for them." Clara remembered how wet her own wings had been during the Valentine's games last year. "And frozen wings break right off!"

"It would have to get a lot colder before our wings broke off," said Silver, laughing. "But we'll be careful!"

Silver helped Lily take off her wings and Lily helped with Silver's.

"Are you coming, Rosie?" Lily asked.

"I'm just bundling up little Squeakie," said Rosie. "Your wings are too little to worry about, aren't they, Squeak?"

"*Hmph*," said Squeak.

"*Hmph*?" said Rosie and she laughed. "I thought that was Lily's favourite word."

"*Hmph*," said Lily. "That's not my favourite word. And besides, Squeak could be saying anything."

Rosie wasn't so sure that was true. She was the closest to Squeak, looking after her every day and watching her grow and change. She had never heard a word from Squeak that she could not understand.

"Come on," said Lily. "Let's get outside before the winds pick up again."

The Fairy Bell sisters trudged out the front door of their fairy house – but they didn't get far before they all sank into the fresh snow.

"It's all the way over my knees!" said Silver. "Watch this!"

She stood up straight as a board and then fell backwards. "Keep your legs together!" shouted Lily. "That's the way to make a perfect snow fairy."

"I already know that!" said Silver. She spread her arms wide and fluttered them up and down. "Come on, Lily. You make one too. And you too, Rosie. And Squeak! Tink will see them in our fairy garden when she flies overhead. One week exactly from today!"

The four Fairy Bell sisters made dozens of snow fairies on their white-blanketed lawn.

"Look at Squeakie's!" said Rosie. She went over to where Squeak's snow fairy was. "How did you make those wings so big, Squeak, with those tiny arms you have? Your snow fairy looks as if she's going to get up and fly away."

"Silver! Lily! Is that you? Everything's so white I can barely see!"

"That's Poppy!" said Silver. "And Avery is right behind her."

The Fairy Bell sisters were friends with everyone on the island, but Poppy and Avery were special. Poppy was Silver's best friend – through thick and thin – and Avery was Lily's. The two fairies landed with a soft thud just next to the Bell sisters' snow fairies.

"These are beautiful," said Poppy. "Oh, and look at Squeakie's! Want to come with us? We're going to pick out our Christmas trees at the Christmas tree forest."

Avery brandished a rather fierce-looking axe. "I know how to chop wood from when I worked on the mainland.

Caraway Cooke sent me this so I could chop down the biggest tree on the island."

"Well, keep it away from me!" said Lily.

"The biggest tree on the island is as tall as a mountain," said Rosie. "But that will be good for cutting down the kind of trees we need."

"Come on, let's go!" said Silver.

"Wait!"

Clara's voice rang out from the front door of the fairy house. "Rosie, Silver Lily – we promised Tink we would let her do everything." Even as Clara said the words she wanted to take them back. She loved choosing their Christmas tree each year and wanted to go with the other fairies to do just that. But she didn't want to disappoint Tinker Bell – not when Tink hadn't been home for Christmas in so long. "That includes choosing the tree."

Silver's face fell. Lily's mouth turned down at the corners. Even Rosie looked disappointed.

"That's right," said Silver at last. "We promised Tink."

All five Fairy Bell sisters sighed a big sigh. It was Rosie who turned the moment bright again. "We didn't promise we wouldn't help our friends!" she said. "Come on everybody, let's go pick out some Christmas trees! You too, Clara. Come on!"

Chapter Six

The Fairy Bell sisters and their friends
flew up to Cathedral Pines, where Ginny
and Genny, the Root Sisters, planted
trees every year for the Christmas tree
forest. The trees above them were
dizzyingly tall.

"None of those, of course," said
Poppy. "They're way too big. Ginny and
Genny will have some just our size."

They flew over to a field of fairy-sized

Christmas trees.

"They'd all be perfect for us," whispered Silver when she saw them.

"Tink will pick a gorgeous tree for you," said Poppy. "The trees in Neverland are probably made of emeralds!"

"With Peter Pan's own arrowheads for decoration!" Silver said, and the two friends grinned.

"Faith told me to pick whichever tree I like best for the classroom," said Avery. She started strolling through the rows of trees with Lily at her side. "We have to make it look jolly for the Christmas Fair."

Avery lived with her teacher, Faith Learned, above the Fairy School. Every

year the Christmas Fair was held there. "I can't wait to do my Christmas shopping at the fair," Avery said. "On the mainland, the shops got so crowded – and I didn't have any way to pay for presents."

"That's so not fair!" said Silver.

"I still can't believe that Queen Mab hands out sparkling stones – for free," said Avery. She had grown up on the mainland and things were very different there.

"Of course she does," said Lily, looking up at a Norway spruce. "We get twelve each. Wait until you see how polished they are, Avery. I hope I get all green this year. Just like my eyes!"

"I like that we each get twelve stones," said Rosie as she ran her hand along the soft needles of a Scots pine. "It's always more than enough to pay for what we'd like to buy—"

"I actually think *fifteen* stones would be better—" said Lily.

"—and anything we can't buy, we make ourselves," said Rosie.

"Tink did say we're not to buy any presents for each other," said Clara. She didn't like always being the one to remind her sisters about what Tink had said, but in fairness, she felt she had to.

"Because we'll get *so* many from her. I bet she'll raid Captain Hook's pirate ship for treasure!" said Silver.

"What do you think your presents from Neverland will look like, Lily?" asked Avery. "I can't even begin to imagine."

Lily didn't answer right away. She was still a tiny bit peeved that Tink was going to bring their tree from Neverland. Lily had very particular ideas about what a Christmas tree should look like. Last year she told Rosie, "It should be taller than a fairy, shorter than a troll, a perfect triangle from top to bottom with soft green needles and a gorgeous sprucy smell to fill up the house." As that thought crossed her mind, she saw the absolutely most perfect Douglas fir tree right ahead of her. "Oh, this is the most beautiful tree on Sheepskerry!" she said. "It belongs in our fairy house."

"Except we're getting an emerald tree, from Neverland!" said Silver.

"Silver, sometimes you are so childish," said Lily. "They don't have emerald trees in—"

"Ooh, that's gorgeous!" said a voice that came from just behind Lily and Silver. "We call that one for us!" And with that, Judy Jellicoe and her sister, Julia, swooped down into the forest next to Lily's tree.

"Oh no!" said Lily.

"Not to worry, Lily," said Rosie. But before Rosie could even give Lily a hug, dozens of Sheepskerry fairies filled the

air and started to choose their Christmas
trees.

"We call this one!" said Acorn Oak.
"It's so pretty and we'll hang it with all
our golden acorn caps."

"We call this one!" said the Shepherd sisters together.

On and on it went until the Christmas tree forest was just about empty. The Fairy Bell sisters watched the trees being cut down one by one. "We've been *robbed*," said Lily.

"Well, not really," said Clara. "Sheepskerry Island is pretty full of trees."

"Not trees that have been specially grown for Christmas," said Lily. "Just straggly old leftovers. What if Tink forgets to bring us one?"

"What if she gets home and finds there's a tree already there?" asked Rosie, although to tell the truth, she had been thinking the same thing. "Tink's been away so long. Let's give her a chance to do something she wants to do for us."

"It's only another few days until Tink comes," said Silver. "We can wait that long, I know we can." She gave her sisters a bright smile. "Let's at least get our decorations out of the attic, in case she needs them to decorate," she said.

Silver's enthusiasm was catching.

"Good idea," said Clara. "And how about a cup of peppermint tea to help us sort them all out?"

"Race you!" said Silver. "And we'll get home faster than any of the other fairies since we don't have to lug home a big old Christmas tree!"

Silver shot off with Lily right behind her. Clara and Rosie, with Squeak squirming in her baby sling, followed a little more slowly.

"Silver's full of Christmas spirit," said

Rosie. "I hope Tink makes it a wonderful Christmas for her."

"I hope so too," said Clara. But inside she added, *Mostly I hope she doesn't disappoint us all.*

 # Chapter Seven

"Ooh, it is so spooky up here!"

Silver (who had won the race, of course) pulled down the trap door to the fairy house attic and peeked into the dark. "We'll use a jellyfish lantern so we can see, but do be careful, Silver," said Clara. "I meant to clear this out last spring but I didn't manage to find the time. And don't let Ginger up here – we'll never find her if she decides to hide."

Lily followed Clara up the steep steps to the attic. She didn't get to go up into the attic nearly as much as she liked to. She immediately flew over to the musty old dressing-up box and opened its creaky lid. "This old-fashioned fairy dress is my favourite," said Lily. "It suits me to a T."

"We're not here to try on clothes, Lily," Clara said. "We're here to fetch the Christmas decorations." She lifted her lantern and the light shone on a dusty corner of the room. Silver zipped up the stairs with Rosie right behind her, carrying Squeak.

"There they are!" said Rosie.

In a corner of the attic was a pile of boxes, all marked in different fairy handwriting:

Decorations – special. Decorations – old. *Fairy lights – white. Fairy lights – coloured.* **Sparkly things** (that was in Lily's writing). **Wrapping paper.** *Ribbons.* **Boxes – used.** Boxes – new.

"Do you ever think we have too many things up here?" asked Clara.

"Never!" said Lily and Silver together.

"Where's the star for the top of the tree?" asked Rosie. "Tink will want to put that on when she comes." She moved a pile of boxes. "It's not here with the other Christmas things. I think we put it somewhere so safe last year that we'll never be able to find it."

"Do you think she'll get here even earlier than she said? Tink, I mean," said Silver. "Maybe she'll come tomorrow. There's only a week left until Christmas, you know."

"She said she'd be here early morning on Christmas Eve," said Lily, wrapping herself in an old velvet cape.

"Don't get your heart set on seeing Tink early," said Clara.

"We'll see her when we see her," said Silver. "I know."

"Help me carry down these boxes, Lily," said Rosie. "I can't manage them all."

"I'll be right there," said Lily. She was trying on the spun-gold cloth that the Fairy Bell sisters wrapped around the base of their Christmas tree every year. "I think this could make a nice skirt for me."

"That's a tree skirt, not a fairy skirt," said Clara. "Tink brought it from Neverland when you were a baby, Lily."

"I've always loved it," Lily said. "It really should belong to me."

"It really should belong to all of us, which it does," said Clara. She held the gold cloth up to the light. "Tink said that this cloth came from Captain Hook's pirate chest. There's nothing else like it in the whole world."

"The other thing there's nothing like in the whole world is Tink's star," said Rosie. "We can't go down without it. Where can it be?"

If any of you are wondering why the fairies celebrate Christmas with so many familiar customs – stars and trees, decorations and presents – let me tell you why. Fairies and humans once

mingled much more than they do now.
As the ages passed, some traditions
of the season were passed down from
human people to the fairies, some
from the fairies to human people. On
Sheepskerry Island at least, it was hard
to tell which was which.

"*Doo!*"

"Squeakie! How did you get there?"

Squeak was all the way over at the
other side of the attic, where the fairies
kept the wicker chairs they hoped to
mend one day.

"You've found the star. And it is pretty,
you're right!"

Squeak was holding up a box marked
FRAGILE! Tink's star. "Good

job, Squeak," said Rosie, taking it from
her carefully. "I love this so much. Tink
made it when I was just a little wee fairy
like you."

Tinker Bell's star may be like the star you have on your own Christmas tree, but it may not be.

"Stars aren't really pointy," she'd said when she made it, so many fairy years ago. "I've seen them up close. And shooting stars are the best of all."

The Bell sisters loved their shooting star. It was so different from the ones on any other fairy trees.

"That's why Tink is so… marvellous," said Silver. "She thinks of things we would never think of."

"All I can think of right now is a nice hot bath," said Lily. "This attic is so dusty."

"Don't use all the bubble bath," said Silver.

"There would be a lot more left if you hadn't tried to wash Ginger with it," said Lily. "I'll use as much as I want."

"Oh, no you don't!" said Silver as she chased Lily down the attic stairs.

"I think this may go on all night," said Rosie. "They're both so excited about Christmas."

"You know what, Rosie?" said Clara. "I'm beginning to get a good feeling about all this. Maybe Tink will even surprise us and arrive tomorrow morning."

"I hope she does, Clara," said Rosie. "Oh, I hope she does."

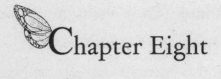# Chapter Eight

But Tinker Bell did not arrive the next day. Nor the day after that. With only five days left until Christmas, every other fairy family was preparing for the big day. The Fairy Bell sisters could not help but feel left out.

And today was the Christmas Fair. Faith Learned's great-great-grandfairy started this Sheepskerry Island tradition long ago. The Fair was a grand

celebration of all the fairies' talents.
Every fairy brought along something
lovely or useful or just plain fun to sell at
the tables lined up in the schoolhouse.
As far back as early autumn, the
Fairy Bell sisters had worked on their
contribution: pretty wind chimes, made
from sea glass hung from
driftwood with silver wires.

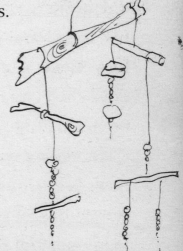

The morning of the
Fair, over a breakfast of
porridge with currants
and cinnamon, with their
steaming cocoa in their
mugs, the sisters arrived
at a decision.

"I know Tink doesn't

want us get each other presents for Christmas," said Clara carefully, "but I don't think she'd want us to go to the Christmas Fair just to look."

"I don't either!" said Lily. "I absolutely *live* for the Christmas Fair!"

"What's your idea, Clara?" asked Rosie.

"Tink would want us to have the best Christmas Fair we could possibly have, so let's be each other's Secret Christmas Fairy."

"Secret Christmas Fairy?" asked Silver. "How does that work?"

"Don't you know anything?" said Lily.

"Lily, please," said Clara. "I'll write all our names on different pieces of paper," said Clara, "like so."

Clara
Rosie
Lily
Silver

Clara wrote her sisters' names on
separate pieces of paper in her best
writing, except for Squeakie's of course.
"That's because we'll each get a little
something for Squeakie," she said. She
put the names into a pointy gnome's hat,
left over from the Valentine's Games.

"Everybody choose one name," she
said to her sisters.

"Then we each get a present for that

sister?" asked Silver.

"Exactly," said Clara.

"A secret present?" asked Silver.

"Yes, you ninny," said Lily.

"Lily, be fair," said Clara. She turned to Silver. "Yes, Silver, a secret present," said Clara. "Nothing too fancy or big."

"It could be *quite* fancy," said Lily.

"Just a tiny little present to keep us going," said Rosie. "Tink won't mind that and if she does I'll give her a piece of my mind." Clara and Rosie looked at each other. "Or not."

"Silver," said Clara, "you draw the first name, since you're the youngest except for baby Squeak."

"*O-deo!*" said Squeak.

"Well you are the baby of the family, Squeak, although someday I suppose you'll be grown."

Silver dipped her hand into the gnome's hat. *I hope I get Rosie*, she thought. She opened up the scroll and read the name.

"Don't say it aloud!" said Lily.

Silver looked at her Secret Christmas Fairy name: *Lily*. Her face only fell a little bit.

"I'm next!" said Lily. "I hope I get my own name. Then I can get myself exactly what I want."

"If you get your own name you have to throw it back," said Clara.

"*Hmph*," said Lily.

She scooped up a name and opened it quickly. *Silver*, it said. "I guess I can live with that," said Lily, "if I have to." Silver could be so annoying, but Lily did love her deep down.

"Your turn, Rosie," said Clara.

Rosie put her hand into the gnome's

hat. Rosie's paper said *Clara*. Rosie smiled.

"That leaves me," said Clara. And of course, as there was only one name left, Clara chose the paper that said *Rosie*. She could think of so many things Rosie would like.

Just then the clock on the mantelpiece chimed twice.

"The Christmas Fair starts in half an hour!" said Lily. "Let's go!"

Chapter Nine

The Fairy Bell sisters flew through the crisp winter wind to Fairy School. They were so happy to glide into the toasty classroom, decorated so cheerily for Christmas. This particular Christmas, Avery and Faith had made the school especially beautiful. They put away anything that made the place look like a classroom, scooping up all the books and maps and charts and hiding them

in the cupboards. Then they pushed
the desks into the centre of the room,
covered them with cloths of gold,
silver and deepest scarlet. The rafters
they strung with lights, the windows
they brightened with candles and in
the corner was their Christmas tree –
decorated with paper chains and a
popcorn garland that the students of
Fairy School had made.

"Can we help?" asked Rosie.

"I think we're just about finished," said
Faith. "Avery made the wreath on the
door – did you see it?"

"I should have known," said Lily. "It
has that Avery touch!"

At that moment, a great cloud of

fairies flew through the door, bringing the cold in with them. Some of them had more items to add to the neatly organised tables. Some were swooping around to see if there were any bargains. All were full of the spirit of the season.

"Can I put my Christmas cookies here?"

"Is there a scarves-and-mittens table?"

"Where do you want us to put decorations?"

"Ooh! Look at the jewellery display!"

Faith was so good at organising and sorting that the Fair was ready to begin. "But I think I'm forgetting something. What can it be?"

"You're forgetting Queen Mab!" Silver said, laughing. "But here she is."

Queen Mab flew in through the classroom doors. There was something more than magical about her, something serene and aglow from inside. All the fairies wanted to grow up to be just like Queen Mab.

"I love what she's wearing!" said Lily.

Queen Mab was dressed in winter

white – not a formal trailing gown, but a much more comfortable outfit that would have been just right for ice skating on Lupine Pond.

"She's really got style," Lily added.

"My dear fairies," Queen Mab said in her lovely clear voice and the crowd hushed. "Welcome, all, to the Christmas Fair." She smiled at all the fairies. "You have done a beautiful job making gifts that express your own skills." She looked around at the jams and jellies from the Jellicoe sisters, the shawls and wraps from the Cobweb sisters, the cushions and pillows from the Stitch sisters, the dried sea lavender from the Flower sisters and the wind chimes from Clara, Rosie, Lily and Silver.

Queen Mab flew high above them all. "Now Lady Courtney will give you each a dozen gems from my own treasure chest, which you can use to buy gifts for family and friends. Lady Courtney, are you ready?"

Indeed she was. The fairies lined up,

all of them in high spirits, laughing and chattering. It took just a few moments for Lady Courtney to distribute the beautiful polished stones to the fairies (everyone helped). Each group of twelve gemstones came in its own small purse.

"They're red this year!" Lily cried when Avery opened hers. "First time!"

"Shall we begin?" asked Queen Mab.

The fairies did not have to be asked twice. Up and down the aisles they flew, looking for the exact right gift for each fairy on their Christmas list.

Chapter Ten

Rosie, with Squeak in her arms, was the first to spot something perfect for her sister.

"Look at that Squeak!"

Squeak just squirmed in her baby sling as Rosie flew over to the Cobweb sisters' table. There

before her was the most beautiful
shawl, spun in an intricate pattern of
hearts and flowers.

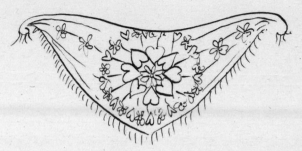

"That's some of my best work," said
Lacey Cobweb.

"It's beautiful," said Rosie. "May I
have it? For Clara?"

"I was hoping you'd spot this for
Clara Bell," said Lacey. "I was thinking
of her as I spun it. It will cost you all
twelve stones. She ran her hand over
the lovely shawl. "But it's a fair price."

"It's worth twice that," said Rosie. She reached into her purse and found only three stones there. "That's funny," said Rosie. "I thought we had twelve stones each."

"We do," said Lacey. "I'm going to buy a necklace for Blanche with my stones – and keep a little for myself so I can buy a silver charm bracelet, too."

"But where are the rest of *my* stones?" said Rosie. "Something must be wrong. I'll fly back to Lady Courtney to see what's up."

Rosie didn't know it, but in another part of the Christmas Fair the same thing was happening.

"I'll take those green and silver

shoelaces for Silver," said Lily as she and Avery looked over everything on the tables.

"She'll love them!" said Avery.

"I know," said Lily. "They'll look so cute in her new trainers."

"Plus they only cost three stones," said Avery, "which leaves you…"

"I think it will leave me enough to buy that darling little skirt from the Stitch sisters. It's almost as pretty as the one in the attic."

"Even if that one is meant for a tree," said Avery. "Wait – you're buying something for yourself?"

"Of course I am!" said Lily. "Silver only likes little things anyway. And half the fun of the Christmas Fair is picking out things I've always wanted!"

Lily had expected to have lots of presents under a gorgeous Christmas tree by now and since there were none she thought it was only fair to treat herself to some little gifts. *It's the least I deserve*, she thought, *waiting so long for Tink to come*!

"Come on, let's see how much you have."

Neither Avery nor Lily was much good at doing maths in their heads, but they could add and subtract very well when they had things they could hold in their hands. So they emptied out Lily's purse to see how many stones would be left when they took three away.

Except there were only three stones in Lily's purse.

Clara was having the same trouble. She had chosen some pretty little coral earrings for Rosie, only to be turned  down by the Seaside sisters when she hadn't enough stones to pay for them.

"You must have spent them somewhere else, Clara," said Shelly Seaside. "Either that or you're trying to trick us into giving you a bargain."

"I'm not trying to trick you!" said Clara, her face hot. "Someone has tricked me!"

"Well, you can have the wire and the posts for three stones, and if you find coral on the beach you can make the earrings yourself. But you may have to bargain with the mermaids for pieces as fine as this – and they're tougher than I am!" Shelly said.

Clara bought the wire and the posts, more out of shame than anything else. She flew over to see Lady Courtney – only to find Rosie and Squeak, Lily and Silver already there.

"Oh dear me!" said Lady Courtney. "I had a feeling something like this was going to happen."

"We only got three measly stones each!" said Lily. She was absolutely

84

fuming. "I bet this is Tink's idea. She thought she'd have some fun with us."

"I knew those purses felt light when I gave them to you. But I had no idea Tink would pull such a trick on us all."

"Our whole Christmas is spoiled," said Lily and she stamped her foot. "All because of Tinker Bell. It's so unfair."

"Don't talk about Tink that way," said Silver. "She's doing the best she can!" But Silver herself was close to tears.

Queen Mab flew over to see what was upsetting the Fairy Bell sisters. "What is it, fairies?" she asked. "It's not like you to be sad at Christmastime."

Lady Courtney told her what Tink had done. "Which is why they got twelve stones between them," she concluded. "In fact, I think Tink has already sent the leftover stones to the poor fairies on the mainland. There was a note in the bottom of the treasure chest about it."

86

Now the Fairy Bell sisters felt really bad. They had so wanted the stones for themselves. But now Tink had sent the leftover stones to the poor fairies, who needed them so much more than they did.

"Fairy Bells," said Queen Mab, "Tink is asking much of you. Possibly too much. I can fetch some more gemstones from my treasure chamber. Shall I?"

Clara looked at her sisters. All of them were so sad, especially poor Lily, who adored shopping.

Silver spoke at last. "Can we get through this… together?" she asked. "For Tink?"

Lily blinked her eyes. Hard. "Maybe," she said in a small voice.

"I think we can," said Clara. "We only wanted to get a few small trinkets for each other to put under the tree—"

"Which we don't have," added Lily.

"Three stones is still a lot," said Silver. "Pretty much, anyway."

"You can't get much with three stones," said Lily, "even if they are polished."

"Let's go back and see what we can find," said Clara. She wanted to be brave for her sisters, but she thought it was very hard on them, very hard indeed. "Come on, sisters. The spirit of the season isn't really about presents, anyway, is it?"

Lily nodded, but she wasn't so sure.

"Let's sing a song to help us through," said Rosie.

"That's a good idea, Rosie. I think if you start a Christmas carol, all the fairies might join in," said Queen Mab. "It would be just the right way to end the Christmas Fair. And perhaps, to cheer up some fairy sisters who don't deserve to be sad."

It wasn't easy to sing with such heavy hearts. "What shall we sing?" asked Clara.

"Something festive," said Queen Mab. "I think it will cheer us all up."

The Fairy Bell sisters gathered close to each other and, wrapping their arms around each other, they began to sing.

They faltered a little at first, finding
the note, but soon their voices joined
together, strong and true:

Deck the halls with boughs of holly
Fa-la-la-la-la, la-la-la-la.
'Tis the season to be jolly
Fa-la-la-la-la, la-la-la-la.
Spread our wings in fair apparel,
Fa-la-la, fa-la-la, la-la-la.
Trill the ancient island carol,
Fa-la-la-la-la, la-la-la-la.

By the time they had sung the first
verse, they felt a bit better. The nice
thing was that all the other fairies
stopped their Christmas shopping and

joined in on the next two verses. So, by the time they reached the last verse, there was a great chorus of voices making a joyful noise and the Fairy Bell sisters' spirits lifted high.

Fa-la-la-la-la, la-la-la-la.

# Chapter Eleven

Everything would have gone pretty well after that, if it hadn't been for Silver.

Silver was following Lily down the aisles of the Christmas Fair to try to get an idea of what she'd really like for Christmas. Silver could think of a hundred things for Lily – she liked so much! – but with only three stones to use, she didn't want to waste a single one. Maybe she'd get three pairs of

92

lacy socks from the Cobweb sisters or
a bracelet from the Gemstone sisters (if
she could afford it) or...

Just then, Silver saw Lily holding up a
green-and-orange bandanna.

"This would be perfect!" she said to
Avery.

They were both giggling.

Does Lily really want that old bandanna for a Christmas present? Silver thought. Then she heard Lily say, "It goes with everything. Too bad I don't have any stones left to buy it for myself."

That was all Silver needed. She swooped down to the table as soon as Lily turned the corner and picked up the bandanna Lily had been holding.

"How much for this?" she asked Fern Stitch.

Fern checked her price list. "That's three stones," she said. "It used to be four, but since the Fair is almost over…"

Silver couldn't really believe she'd have to pay her only three stones for this not-very-nice bandanna, but… "This is what Lily wants," said Silver. "And since Lily's the only one I'm buying a present for—"

"The only one?" said Fern. "Why aren't you getting presents for your other sisters? Did you have a fight? That doesn't sound like you!"

"Of course we didn't have a fight. It's just that – well, Tinker Bell kind of changed the rules this Christmas."

At the sound of Tink's name, several fairies stopped to hear the news from Neverland.

"Tink changed the rules? What do you mean? Is she hoping to get here this year?"

"Hoping! She didn't say hoping,"

said Silver. She didn't want the other
fairies thinking that Tink would leave
them hanging. "Tink says she's coming
on the morning of Christmas Eve with
our tree and our decorations and all
our presents." By this time Silver was
grinning wide. She remembered how
fantastic Christmas would be once Tink
arrived. "She's been away so long and
now she's coming home."

"Oh we can't wait to meet her!" said Fern. Many of the fairies on Sheepskerry had only heard of Tinker Bell in books. They gathered around now.

"You can all meet her," said Silver. "You can all come over when she arrives. We'll have a huge surprise party for her!"

"Silver, what are you talking about?" said Clara who had flown by to see why the crowd was forming around her little sister. "We're not having—"

"Oh yes we are," said Silver. "We're having a huge surprise party at four o'clock on Christmas Eve. You're all invited! And Tink will be the guest of honour."

Chapter Twelve

I'm sure I don't need to tell you that Silver had acted a little too quickly. She got an earful from Clara about remembering to *check with her sisters* before she did something like that again. But Clara couldn't be upset with Silver for long. Silver was so excited about Tink's arrival that adding another ten or twelve fairies to the mix didn't seem such a bad idea.

As Rosie had said, "This is turning

out to be such a topsy-turvy Christmas
I won't be surprised, no matter what
happens."

So on the morning before Christmas,
the great room at the Fairy Bell sisters'
house looked far from sad, even though
there was no tree in the bay window
and no wreath on the door. The presents
the sisters had made for Tink and
bought for each other at the Christmas
Fair were wrapped in cheery paper and
set out on the windowsill. Poppy came
over that morning to help Silver gather
holly branches to place in the rafters.

"Tink won't mind that," said Poppy.

"Tink won't mind anything!" said
Silver. "She'll be so surprised when she

gets here and finds all her fairy friends.
She'll make the party such a magical
event!"

"I'm sure it will be lovely whether Tink
is here or not," said Poppy. "You sisters
have done so much already."

"Oh, but Tink will put the magical
touches on it all," said Silver. "Without
her it's just an ordinary tea party, but
with her – it's completely special."

Silver and Poppy cut as many holly
branches as they could manage without
getting too scratched by the pointy
leaves. They flew back to the Fairy Bell
sisters' fairy house with some difficulty.
Not only were the branches heavy in
their arms, but the wind was blowing

quite fiercely.

"That wind is really kicking up again," said Poppy. "I hope it won't blow Tink off course."

"Tink is so close to Sheepskerry by now that a little wind won't hurt," said Silver, even as she and her best friend

had to fight the gusts. "She'll be here in lots of time for the party. You wait and see."

Wait and see. Silver wished she had never said those words. Because waiting and waiting and waiting and *not* seeing was exactly what she and Poppy did that day. It wasn't so bad at breakfast time, as they knew Tinker Bell would not arrive in time for an early meal. But Tink had said the morning of Christmas Eve and as the clock got closer and closer to noon, Silver's heart sank.

"The other fairies will be coming for our Welcome Home Tink party so soon!" Silver cried as the clock struck three. "She hasn't even arrived yet. We won't get to see her for more than a few minutes before everybody else arrives. It's not fair!"

"We might not get to see her at all at this rate," said Lily. "I wouldn't be surprised if she just forgot—"

"Don't say such a thing, Lily," said Rosie, who was almost never cross. But between all this waiting for Tinker Bell and Squeakie's fussing and Silver's chatter, even Rosie's nerves were frayed.

"Yes, please, Lily. Things are difficult enough today, now that Silver has invited a dozen fairies to a magical tea."

"Now it's turned into *twenty* fairies and I'll say what I want," said Lily. "And it will probably turn out to be thirty fairies or more. All our fairy friends are bringing their fairy friends. We have about enough sandwiches and cakes for ten. Tink had better get here and get here fast." And she flew up to her bedroom and slammed the door.

"I'm not feeling very Christmassy," said Silver.

"*No lolo*," said Squeak.

"That's about the first thing she's said that I've really understood this whole week," said Rosie. "What do you suppose is going on with her?"

"Can you please stop talking about Squeak when I'm the one who needs love and care?" said Silver. "No one is paying attention to me!" And she flew up to her room.

"We can't pay attention to you and take care of Squeak and make a party for twenty—"

"Thirty!" Silver shouted.

"Thirty fairies at the same time!" said Clara. "Stop feeling sorry for yourself and get down here and help."

If you have a brother or sister or know someone who does, you'll understand exactly what was going on at the Fairy Bell sisters' house just then. Silver was bitterly disappointed that Tink had not yet arrived. Lily was still unhappy about not getting that skirt at the Christmas Fair. Rosie was preoccupied with Squeakie and Clara was suddenly in charge of a party she did not want to give. In short, all the Fairy Bell sisters were upset and even a little bit angry and they were pretty much taking it out on each other.

Ding-dong! The doorbell of the fairy house rang out.

"I'll get it!" said Poppy, glad to have something to do.

"If that is the Jellicoe sisters I will just about have a fit," said Clara. "They always come early."

The front door opened and in flew Judy and Jilly Jellicoe. "We're here!" cried Judy.

"We were going to bring some jelly beans for the tea but Silver said not to

bring a thing."

"Of course you weren't to bring a thing," said Clara smoothly. "We have everything just about prepared. Why don't you take off your coats and hats while I get the party food from the kitchen."

"You are ready for us, aren't you?" asked Julia. "I know we're a little bit on

the early side but I have to say it looks like—"

"It looks like we are absolutely ready," said Silver, flying down from her room with her eyes only slightly red. Lily and Rosie followed right behind her. When anyone else made them feel bad, the Fairy Bell Sisters always rallied around each other, which was exactly what they were doing now.

"Welcome!" said Lily.

"We're so pleased to have you," said Rosie.

"*Bo-bo!*" said Squeak.

The doorbell rang again (and again) and lots more fairies showed up.

"Where's Tinker Bell?"

"Is she visiting Queen Mab?"

"What did she bring you from Neverland?"

"Where's that tree with crystal branches?"

"I heard they were emerald."

Clara, Rosie, Lily and Silver fended off the questions as best they could. To tell the truth, having so many fairies there, all needing another glass of blackberry punch or a new plate of pumpkin butter sandwiches, made the time pass much faster than it had all week.

"Tink must get here soon," said Iris Flower, checking the clock on the mantelpiece. "Christmas Eve will be over before you know it."

Indeed the clock was striking the hour of six o'clock, when the fairies usually would go home to be at their own fairy houses and prepare for Christmas morning. But they stayed just a little longer, in case Tink arrived at the last minute.

But she did not.

"We've waited long enough, I think," said Satin Stitch as the last chime of seven o'clock died away. "I'm so sorry Tink didn't manage to come to her own party."

"She's coming!" said Silver fiercely.
"She's just not here yet. You would have
trouble flying from Neverland in this
kind of weather, too!"

No one wanted to stay much longer
after that outburst. Soon the last of the
fairy guests drifted away until it was just
the Fairy Bell sisters and their very best
friends.

"I'm sure she'll be here very soon,"
said Avery as she hugged Lily tight.

"I don't know if I even care any
more," said Lily.

"Of course you do," said Avery. "And
she *will* be here." She flew towards
the door. "Faith and I will come
over tomorrow morning to celebrate

Christmas with you. We'll see you and
your famous sister then."

"I hope so," said Lily.

After Poppy and Silver finally said
their very long goodbyes, there was
nothing left but to clear up and to head
to bed.

"I don't know if I can face these
dishes," said Clara. "I thought all this
would be done by magic. I thought for
once that Tink would—" Clara dropped
a plate on the floor and it broke with a
sharp crack.

"Oh Clara! Don't say it," said Rosie
and she picked up the pieces. "Don't
lose faith in Tinker Bell. She would be
here if she could."

"Then why isn't she?" asked Clara. "Why hasn't she come, Rosie? Why did she have to ruin our Christmas just so she could be the star?"

"That's who she is Clara. And we love so much about her – we have to love that too." Rosie put the dustpan and broom away in the cupboard. Then she hugged her sisters tight. "Let's just leave the dishes for once and go to bed. Maybe Tink will come tomorrow, on Christmas Day."

"And if she doesn't?"

For a moment, Rosie was tempted to say that Clara was right: if Tink didn't arrive, Christmas would be ruined. But then she thought of the way Lily was trying so hard to make do with just a few presents and how Squeakie was struggling to be understood, how Silver had been so brave when the guest of honour did not arrive at her own surprise party and of course of the way Clara held them all together.

"If she doesn't come," said Rosie, "we'll make it the best Christmas we can."

"You know what?" said Clara, taking off her apron. "Let's start right now."

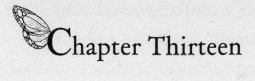Chapter Thirteen

"Silver! Lily!" Clara's voice was brimming with mischief. "Come down here right now."

"What is it, Clara?" asked Rosie.

"You'll see," said Clara.

Silver and Lily came down to the great room in their pyjamas, while Squeakie slept soundly in her cot.

"Tink's not here, is she?" asked Silver.

"Nope, not yet, and let's stop talking

about when she'll come and what she'll bring. Let's celebrate being here together with each other. If she arrives tomorrow it will be lovely to see her. And if she doesn't—"

"If she *doesn't?*" said Silver, her face falling.

"If she doesn't," said Clara firmly, "then we will send her our love and promise to come visit her in Neverland next year."

"We'd go to *Neverland?*" said Rosie.

"Why not?" said Lily. "I wonder what exactly those Lost Boys are like."

"We'll go together and see Tink next year and bring Christmas to her. By next year I should have just about enough magic to get us there."

"Maybe Queen Mab will send us in her Royal Balloon!" said Silver.

"You're right!" said Clara. "But why are we talking about next Christmas, when it's practically Christmas right now? We've got some presents to open!"

"Are you sure Tink won't mind?" asked Silver.

"I'm quite sure," said Clara. "Tink may get distracted and not do everything quite as she hopes to, but I know for a fact she would not want Christmas to be spoiled for us."

"Let's take a vote. All in favour of opening one present right now, say 'aye'!"

"Aye!" said Rosie, Clara and Silver.

"*Yi-yi!*" said Squeak.

"All opposed, say 'nay'!" said Lily.

No one said nay, but Ginger said *Mew* which made them all laugh.

"Then let's begin!" said Lily.

They gathered their small pile of presents around them. In the light of the fire, it looked like a treasure trove.

"Let's go oldest to youngest this time," said Silver. "I want to save mine for last."

Rosie handed Clara a package. "I was your Secret Fairy," she said. "I wrapped it in a tea-towel, see?

"Ooh, I love it, Rosie," said Clara.

"It's part of your present," said Rosie.

Clara secretly hoped that Rosie's entire Secret Fairy gift was not going to be about drying dishes, but she didn't say anything in case that's what Rosie had chosen for her.

When she opened up the tea towel,

she could hardly believe her eyes.

"It's the shawl I wanted, from the Cobweb sisters! Oh Rosie, how did you do that? It cost far more than three polished stones."

"The Cobwebs were kind," said Rosie. "They gave me the pattern and I crocheted it myself. Don't look too closely!" She did not say that she had been up hours every night since the Christmas Fair finishing the shawl for Clara. Her reward was the happiness on Clara's face.

Clara wrapped the shawl around her slender shoulders. Its warm turquoises and corals set off her dark skin and dark eyes.

"You should wear that at the next Valentine's Games!" said Silver. "Rowan won't be able to take his eyes off you!"

"He already has trouble doing that," said Lily.

Clara's cheeks flushed. "How about you, Rosie? Here's one for you! I was your Secret Fairy."

Rosie looked at the tiny package in front of her.

"Three stones are not a whole lot to work with," said Clara.

"Oh, I love tiny packages, you know that Clara," said Rosie. "I just like to take my time." She gave her big sister a hug then unwrapped the little box to find the sweet shell earrings inside.

"This was just what I'd hoped for," she said. "How did you know?"

"I wanted to get you coral, but the mermaids wouldn't help me," said Clara. "I had to make these myself, so if they're a little clumsy, you'll know why."

"I think they're lovely," said Rosie, slipping the earrings on. "I wouldn't have wanted coral, anyway." That was only a little bit of a fib. "These suit me perfectly." She gave Clara a hug. Her big sister loved her so much.

"I know I said I'd go last but can I go next?" asked Silver. "I can't wait any more!"

"Of course you can go next," said Clara. A tree branch rattled against the windowpane. "Just listen to that wind."

"I know. It's really howling," said Rosie. "It almost sounds like a cat or bird or—"

"No one would be out on a night like this, Rosie," said Clara.

Lily handed Silver her present. "It's not much," said Lily. "But I hope you like it."

"This paper is amazing!" said Silver. "It's practically a present itself."

"I designed it myself," said Lily. "It's part of my line."

"Let's see what's inside," said Silver. She peeked into the package. "Oh! It's laces for my fairy running shoes!" she

said. "I love these, I love these," she sang. "They are perfect colours and just what I wanted. I'm going to put them on right now!" She flew over to the entrance hall and fetched her running shoes. The new laces were laced up in no time. "These look great!" said Silver, admiring them on her feet. "Thank you Lily. Merry Christmas!"

Lily began to feel a little bit better about the presents her sisters were getting for Christmas. Maybe Silver, too, had picked out the perfect present at the Christmas Fair. *There were so many things that could have been perfect for me*, she thought.

"Open yours, Lily!" said Silver. "Open yours!"

Lily tore through the wrapping paper, which had been clumsily put on by Silver. "It's just what you wanted, isn't it? You said, you said!"

Lily's face fell. It was the second-hand green-and-orange bandanna. The one she had been making fun of with Avery at the Stitch sisters' stand.

"You really thought I'd like this?" said Lily. She was close to tears.

"At first I didn't really believe that you and Avery would even notice such a thing, but then you talked about it so much I knew you really meant it," Silver said. She was so happy with her gift that she didn't notice Lily's eyes were glistening. "You're so good at

accessorising, Lily. I know you'll make this look fabulous somehow." She gave Lily a big hug. "I'm so happy I could get you exactly what you wanted for Christmas!"

Lily gave Silver a hug back. "Merry Christmas, Silver," said Lily softly.

Clara saw Lily brush away a tear and her heart melted. She whispered something to Silver, who whispered to Rosie, who nodded.

"What is it?" asked Lily.

"Wait there just one minute…" said Silver. She flew over to the stack of Christmas decorations laid out for Tinker Bell and pulled something out from the bottom. "It's the second part of your

present," said Silver, her face shining.
"We're giving you the Christmas tree
skirt, Lily!"

"But that belongs to everyone," said
Lily.

"Not now!" said Clara.

"Try it on, Lily," said Rosie.

"Really?" asked Lily.

"Yes please!" said her sisters.

Lily whipped the golden Christmas
tree skirt around her waist. She tied
a bow at the back. The golden fabric
glowed in the firelight and caught the
light in Lily's long hair.

The sisters had seen that tree skirt
around the Christmas tree for years, but
on Lily it took on new life.

"You're gorgeous!"
said Clara simply.

"Oh thank you!"
cried Lily. "Thank
you all!"

The four Fairy
Bell sisters sat in
the glow of the
dying fire. There was
no tree, only a few
gifts, no Christmas feast and Tink had
not come. And yet, this was the best
Christmas they had ever had.

"Shall we get ready for bed now?"
asked Clara. "Tomorrow's Christmas
Day. We'll visit everyone in the fairy
village—"

"And we'll feast at Queen Mab's palace," said Silver.

"And we'll help Squeakie open all her presents, when she wakes up bright and early. Won't we Squeak?"

The sisters got up to look into Squeak's fairy cot.

"She must have been awfully tired. I haven't heard a peep from her for ages," said Clara.

"Are you asleep, Squeak? asked Rosie softly. "Or are you—"

Rosie let out a gasp.

"Oh no! Oh no!" she cried. "Squeak's gone!"

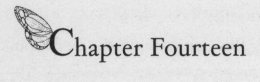

Chapter Fourteen

Clara, Rosie, Lily and Silver looked all over their fairy house for baby Squeak. They did not find her. Anywhere.

"She cannot have gone far. She must be hiding somewhere to play a trick on us. Squeak, come on, now, it's not funny any more. Where are you?"

"She's not here, Clara," said Rosie. "I can feel it. She's gone. I don't know how or what has happened, but she has gone."

"If she's gone she can't have gone far. She's too tiny. She must have crawled under one of the beds. Silver, go and check again."

Silver flew upstairs to the bedrooms but Rosie felt in her fairy wingtips that something was not right. Squeak had been acting so strangely for the past few weeks.

"I should have known something was the matter with her. What did she want me to know?" Rosie's wings kept quivering. "She was trying to tell me something. But what?"

Some instinct made Rosie go to the back door of the fairy house. "Clara, look. It's open a crack. She went outside

for some reason. Oh, it's freezing out there."

Clara took one step out the door and knew Rosie was right. It was freezing outside. In fact the temperature had been dropping all evening. "We have to find her!" said Clara.

She, Rosie, Lily and Silver gathered what hats and coats they could find and rushed out the back door, Lily with a lantern in hand.

"Follow her tracks in the snow!" said Silver. "Look! I see them! We'll find her in no time now!"

None of the sisters wanted to say what they were all thinking. It was bitterly cold out on Sheepskerry Island, with the wind whipping and the snow swirling. A little baby fairy could not get far.

"Here are her little footsteps!" said Silver. "They're heading straight out our front garden to—"

Silver stopped short. The tracks had disappeared. "There's nothing else here," said Silver. "It's as if… she disappeared."

Lily, Clara and Rosie rushed over to where Silver stood. "Those are her footsteps," said Lily. "But where did she go from here?"

"Did someone come and fetch her?" asked Clara.

"No, they would have brought her back home," said Rosie.

"Did she fall and hurt herself?" Silver asked.

"There's no sign of that," said Clara.

"Then where oh where can she be?" Rosie cried.

Silver leaned down and looked carefully at the footsteps in the snow. "Look everybody," she said, "they get closer together right here."

"And then... nothing," said Rosie.
She was on the verge of panicky tears.
"It's almost like someone snatched her
away."

"Or..." said Clara, "as if she flew."

Chapter Fifteen

Once the Fairy Bell sisters realised that Baby Squeak might be able to fly, they were filled with wonder and relief – and even more panic. Where could she have gone? And why?

"Let's calm down and use our heads," said Clara.

"We can look for flying tracks," said Silver. "She's flying but she can't be completely sure of herself yet. She must have left tracks in the trees."

Sure enough, Silver was right. The sisters looked up at the trees right above Squeak's last footprints.

"Look!" Lily said. "Heading toward the east shore! The branches are broken."

"Lily's right. She must have started this way. And— Oh look, some more footprints!"

Bit by bit, the Fairy Bell sisters followed Squeakie's clumsy trail through the fairy village, around Sunrise Hill, in the direction of the fairy library.

"I can't believe how far she flew," said Rosie. "Where could she be going?"

"I think she must be looking for Tink," said Clara.

"I don't think that's it," said Rosie. "She was trying to tell me something, but I didn't listen. Oh, Squeakie – I am so sorry!"

"We all could have listened better," said Lily. She hated to see Rosie upset. "But we can't dwell on that. We need to find her. Oh look!" her eyes lit up. "She landed here. You can tell by the snow!"

Indeed, there was a big dent in the snow beyond the fairy library over near the east shore. "Squeakie! Are you here? Where did you go?"

Then they heard something.

"What was that?" said Clara. "An owl?"

"There won't be any owls out on such a cold night," said Silver. She drew her

138

jacket around her.

The strange cry came again.

"A cat?" asked Lily.

"Ginger is safe at home," said Silver.
"And Poppy wouldn't let Lucky out on a
night like this."

The sisters listened again.

"That's not Squeak's voice, I know
that much," said Rosie. "It's that cry I
heard before, when we were opening
our presents. It sounds more like—"

"Look – over there on Heart Island! Can you see something?"

Clara, Rosie, Lily and Silver strained their eyes as they looked over onto the little island off Sheepskerry's east shore.

"I think I see her!" cried Rosie. "I think she's there on Heart Island."

"What is she doing there?" said Lily. "Did she run away from home?"

"Squeakie would never run away from home," said Clara. "Something must be up. Come on, sisters, we have no time to lose." Clara could feel her wings starting to freeze. And if her wings were freezing, Squeak's must be freezing too.

Chapter Sixteen

Rosie knew they were lucky – the wind
was coming from the west and blew
them over to Heart Island with no wear
and tear on their wings, which were
stiff from the cold. *How we'll get back is
anyone's guess*, Rosie thought. "Oh, why
didn't we stop to ask for Queen Mab's
help?"

"We didn't have time," Clara replied.
"We did the right thing." Clara didn't

even want to think about what might have happened if they hadn't acted as quickly as they had.

"She's right in the middle of the island," said Silver. "I can still hear that cry—"

"It's a cat, I think," said Lily.

"Whatever it is, the sound is coming from the middle of the island. Not much further now."

In the very middle of Heart Island, there's a rock that looks like a heart itself. At the top of the rock there's a little cleft, which makes a shelter. That's where the noise was coming from. And that's where the Fairy Bell sisters found Squeakie Bell.

"Oh Squeak! You're all right!" cried Clara. "You're all right!"

All the Fairy Bell sisters rushed over to give her a hug. And I don't mind telling you: many tears were shed.

"Why did you leave us?"

"How did you fly so far?"

Then the little cry came again. "What's making that noise, Squeak?"

They looked carefully. Squeak was

sitting in the shelter of the rock, and
nestled in her lap was something even
smaller than she was.

"What have you got there, Squeak?"
asked Clara.

Rosie was the first to realise. "Oh my!"
said Rosie. "The question is not *what*
have you got there. It's *who* have you
got there?"

And Squeak said, "Baby."

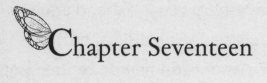

Chapter Seventeen

"Squeak! You said a word!" said Lily. "You said 'baby'!"

"A real word," said Clara. "Oh Squeakie, we are so proud of you!"

"Not to mention you rescued a new baby fairy!" said Silver.

It didn't take long for the Fairy Bell sisters to figure out what had happened. (Nor you, I'm sure!) Squeak had been out of sorts because her wings ached

146

from learning to fly. Her sisters hadn't thought it possible that she'd be flying so early – most fairies don't learn until they're five fairy years old and Squeakie was barely two. Little fairies have a knack for understanding or hearing each other, so it was no wonder that Squeak heard this little fairy's cries despite the wind and the distance.

Most fairy babies are not born in the winter, because it's so cold that human children often are busier keeping themselves warm rather than laughing. (Fairies are born when a human child laughs for the first time, as some of you already know.) And most fairy babies land in a safe place with their sisters

gathered around them… but this one did not.

"Thank goodness she wasn't harmed!" said Clara.

"You saved her life, Squeak," said Rosie.

Now the question was, what to do next?

"Baby," said Squeak again.

"We see, Squeak!" said Silver. "We see it's a new baby." She turned to her sisters. "Shouldn't we get her home?"

The five Fairy Bell sisters looked into the night. The temperature had continued to drop. And the wind was against them. "We flew out here, but we may not be able to fly back!" said Lily. "With this cold, our wings might snap right off."

"We can walk back to the island if it's low tide," said Silver. But one glance at the rocks showed them that the tide had flooded in while the fairies were looking for Squeak. "We can't walk. And we can't fly. And if this baby does not get in out of the snow before long, she might—"

"Don't even say it!" said Rosie. "We have got to get her back to our

fairy house. And Squeakie, too. She's freezing!"

The Fairy Bell sisters looked over at Squeakie and the tiny fairy baby. The temperature was way below freezing. The wind was bitter. But since there was no proper shelter on Heart Island the only way to safety was to fly home. Fast.

"Squeak's teeth are chattering. Oh, Squeakie, what possessed you to come out in this tiny little fairy dress? And no coat or hat?"

"Baby," said Squeak.

"I know!" said Rosie. "You wanted to take care of the baby. And that was just the right thing to do. But now how will we take care of you?"

Clara pulled off the shawl Rosie had just given her for Christmas. "Let's wrap you up, Squeak, and the baby too." Clara tried to wrap the two little fairies in her new shawl, but the baby was too squirmy to keep it on, so it kept falling off Squeakie, too.

"Tear it in half, Clara," said Rosie. "It's the only way to keep them both warm!"

"But you worked so hard on it!" said Clara.

"It doesn't matter now," said Rosie. "These little ones need it more than any of us. I'll make you another, Clara, but not in time for Christmas!"

Without wasting another moment, Clara began tearing Rosie's carefully

crocheted stitches on a rock. Then she ripped the beautiful shawl in two. "I'm sorry Rosie!" said Clara. But Rosie was already busy wrapping up the baby in one half of the shawl so Clara wrapped Squeak in the other.

"Their teeth aren't chattering any more," said Silver. "Hold them close! I think they're going to be OK!"

"But how will we get off Heart Island and back to Sheepskerry?" said Clara. She tentatively stretched out a wing. The wind had died down and the temperature seemed to be holding steady. "I think we have a few minutes to get across without snapping our wings off," she called. "But I don't know how we'll be able to fly into the wind and hold these little ones at the same time!"

Silver thought of it first. "If we can make some kind of baby slings, you could keep the baby safe, Rosie. And

Clara can hold Squeakie the same way. But we have to do it fast." She squinted at the horizon. "It looks like there might be a snowstorm on the way."

"Here!" said Lily. "Use my skirt!"

"We can't do that to you, Lily!" cried Clara.

"These babies need it. We all need it. So let's use it, please!"

"I know!" said Silver. And she whipped the green-and-silver shoelaces out of her new shoes. "We can use these to tie up the baby slings. It's got to work somehow."

"But your feet will freeze without your trainers!"

"I'll hang on to these trainers, don't

worry about that."

In a moment, Lily had torn her skirt into strips and wrapped the baby onto Rosie's chest. "Oh, this won't stay!" cried Lily. "The laces are too slippery to hold a knot like this!"

Without a word, Rosie took off one of her treasured earrings, unbent the wire and twisted it on to her baby sling. "There," said Rosie. "Not as good as a safety pin, but it will hold." She did the same for Clara and Squeakie.

"Do you really think we can get across?" asked Silver. It wasn't like her to be afraid, but the storm was fearsome, the sky dark, the winds fierce, the water beating against the rocks. "If we get weak or tired we may…"

"If we're weak or tired we will pull each other through!" said Lily.

"We can do this, sisters," said Clara.

"We *must* do this to save ourselves," said Rosie. "And to save the…"

She waited for Squeak to say "baby." But Squeak was too weak to say a word.

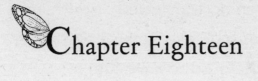# Chapter Eighteen

Out into the fearsome wind they flew.
I can barely imagine how they did it.
There hadn't been quite enough food
at the party so none of them had had
much to eat since their breakfast, hours
and hours ago. Halfway between Heart
Island and Sheepskerry they were blown
back out to sea, which meant their
journey was even longer than it should
have been. They looked in vain for help

from seals or sea birds, but no other
creature was foolish enough to venture
out in this kind of cruel winter wind.

"Hold on, Squeak," said Clara. "Hold
on and we will get you warm and safe
again."

Rosie could tell that the baby fairy was
all right, thanks to the baby sling Lily
had made. Still, she was squirming and
fussing. "Be calm, little one," said Rosie.
"I promise we will keep you safe from
harm." But even as she said the words,

she didn't know if she could keep her promise.

"We have to give her a name!" called Silver as she flew. "Oops, there goes my trainer!"

"Not now, Silver," said Clara.

"Yes now! I've got to take my mind off this wind somehow."

"Okay!" called Rosie over the wind. "She was born one day before Christmas, so something Christmassy."

"Holly?" called Silver.

"Star?" cried Lily.

"Pudding?" asked Rosie.

"Definitely not Pudding," said Lily.

"How about Noel?" said Clara. And even with the wind howling in her ears,

Clara could hear the baby laugh. "Noel it is then," she said in a whisper.

"Land!" cried Silver. "Sheepskerry Island, twenty metres away."

Through the darkness the Fairy Bell sisters could just see the outline of the tall spruce trees on Sheepskerry's shore.

"There's White Rose Cottage!" cried Rosie. She had never been so happy to see a place in her life.

"Shall we stop there and rest?" asked Lily. "I think I can go on, but you two must be exhausted, carrying those little ones."

"Let's press on!" cried Clara. "I can do it now. Can you Rosie?"

"I can!" cried Rosie.

The Fairy Bell sisters put on a final burst of speed and soon were nearly back at their fairy house.

"Oh no, Clara!" cried Rosie. "Our house! What's the matter?"

There was a strange glowing coming from the Bell sisters' fairy house.

It can't be on fire, can it? thought Clara, her heart racing. *Not after all we've been through.*

"Hurry!"

Though their wings were exhausted with effort and their hands and faces raw with the cold, the sisters pushed on to their house.

"If our house is gone, we'll manage somehow," said Rosie. "The Flower sisters will take us in, or Queen Mab."

"But all our pretty things – they can't be burned to the ground, can they?"

As the sisters flew closer and closer to their fairy house the glow only got brighter. But one by one they began to think that perhaps it wasn't fire after all.

"I don't think our house is on fire," said Rosie. "There's no smoke."

"And no flames," said Clara. "But feel how warm it is!"

They landed on the lawn of their fairy house. The house was not on fire. It was lit with a brilliant light from inside. The light was so strong and clear that Squeakie's eyes opened for a moment.

"*Aahma*," she said.

"Open the door, Clara," said Silver. "See if it really is magic."

Clara tentatively put her hand on the doorknob. She turned it gently, and then flung it wide.

The great room was dazzling. Where there had been an empty space, now

there was a giant Christmas tree hung
with every imaginable decoration and
Tink's star on top. Where there had been
a few torn pieces of wrapping paper on
the floor, now there was an enormous
pile of presents, teetering almost to the
ceiling. There was a glorious feast on the
table. A wreath above the mantelpiece.
The smell of cinnamon and brown sugar
was in the air. Steaming mugs of hot
chocolate stood on the large oak table.

Even the air of the great room was filled with the sound of delicate bells.

And in the middle of it all stood someone they all knew.

"Oh Tink! Tink!" cried the Fairy Bell sisters all at once. "You've come home. You've come home at last."

# Chapter Nineteen

Oh what a feast they had! What a glorious reunion for all six Fairy Bells! So much love was there in the fairy sisters' house Rosie thought it might burst from all the happiness inside it.

The clock had long since chimed midnight and the sisters could not wait until the morning to celebrate. So they dug in to their feast and opened gift after gift and sang until their voices wore out.

Later, Clara thought there must have been magic involved, because Christmas night seemed to last forever. They finally dropped into bed, exhausted, asleep before their heads sank into their pillows. Tink took care of the tiny new baby fairy and tenderly tucked in Squeakie when she'd finally stopped flying around. "We can't call her Baby Squeakie any more," said Clara.

"Not when there's a new baby in the house," said Silver.

None of the Fairy Bell sisters saw the dawn, but it broke bright and clear. The glow from their house could be seen even in the daylight and soon all the fairies of Sheepskerry came to visit

Tinker Bell and her sisters. Tink led
them in a merry procession to Queen
Mab's palace, where they gathered
for a festival of song and story. Tink
told them tales of Neverland that would
fill a book longer than this one.

Finally, the sun set over the Sheepskerry Bay and Christmas Day was over.

Tink and her sisters said one last farewell.

"Are you really going so soon?" asked Silver.

"Peter Pan's waiting for me," said Tink.

"Come back again soon, Tink!" said Clara.

Tinker Bell kissed each of her sisters (and baby Noel) in turn. Then she raised her wings and flew away.

Where Tink had stood, a trail of sparkles swirled in her place.

"There's one last Christmas surprise for you," they chimed. "Can't wait until you discover it!"

As Clara turned and went back into the fairy house she thought she would be lonely without her big sister Tinker Bell there. But the house was so full of love and magic that Tink's glow wrapped around them all and filled them with even more joy.

"I suppose we should get ready for bed," said Clara. "It's been such a long day."

"I'm so tired I could absolutely drop," said Lily, admiring her new skirt of spun gold. Tinker Bell had magicked her a

new one, from Neverland. "I wonder if I can wear this to bed."

"I'd wear these trainers to bed if I could," said Silver. "They'll make me go even faster than the ones I lost – or the one I lost, I should say." Tink had made new trainers appear by magic for her little sister.

Rosie took the sweet coral earrings from her ears and laid them carefully on her dressing table. "Tink knows just what I like," said Rosie as she tucked Squeakie in.

"Baby?" said Squeakie.

"Clara's taking care of our new baby sister, Squeak," said Rosie. "Don't you worry." Rosie called to her older sister as she started work on a new shawl for her, "Have you found the stack of clothes Tink laid out for her?"

"I have!" called Clara. "What an odd assortment she chose, though," she said to herself. "None of Lily's old things and hardly any of Rosie's or mine. They're all bits and pieces from our old dressing-up box. What was Tink thinking?"

Silver, Lily, Rosie and Squeak had just laid their heads on their pillows when a shriek came from Clara downstairs, followed by a great peal of laughter from baby Noel.

"Clara! What is it? Is everything all right?"

"Oh my gosh," said Clara. "I think I've

found that last surprise Tink said we'd discover."

That was enough to get everyone out of bed. The sisters flew down the stairs, Squeak leading the way.

"What is it?" asked Lily. "What's the surprise? More presents?" Even Lily didn't think she could take any more.

"Another baby?" Rosie was only half-kidding.

"Another kitten?" asked Silver. "Or a puppy?"

"I've got news for you," said Clara as she came back with baby Noel freshly cleaned and changed in her arms. "Our new fairy sister... is a boy."

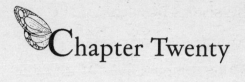

Chapter Twenty

When they stopped exclaiming and wondering and laughing, the Fairy Bell sisters headed to bed, their new baby *brother* fairy taking Squeak's place in the cot in the great room.

"We'll love this little fairy no matter what," said Rosie.

"Boy oh boy, is everyone going to be very surprised," said Silver.

"Boy oh boy is right!" said Lily.

"We just need to give him love and care and a happy home," said Clara.

"That's what all little ones need," said Clara. "That's the recipe for a happy—"

"Baby," said Squeak.

And they went to bed that Christmas night, dreaming of Tinker Bell and Christmas magic and new fairy babies and of all the adventures that lay ahead of them.

FAIRY SECRETS

Squeak's Words

O-bee!– Not me!

Ahhma!– Oh my!

Doo!– Pretty!

Odeo!– Oh dear!

No lolo – Don't be sad.

Bo-bo! – Welcome!

How to Make
Fairy Bell Holiday Punch

The secret of a perfect party? Perfect punch! Here's what the Fairy Bell sisters serve when they're expecting a big crowd. (Ask a grown-up to help.)

4 cups of fairy apple juice made
   from Sheepskerry apples*
1 cup of cranberry juice from fairy
   cranberry bogs*
2 cups of chilled fairy ginger
   ale from the shops on the
   mainland*
A little lemon juice (fairy or non-
   fairy – your choice)

Combine the apple juice, the
cranberry juice, and the lemon juice in
a large bowl. Chill on the back porch
of your fairy house or in a refrigerator.
When the mixture is nice and cold, add
the ginger ale, stir and serve to fairy
friends.

Try adding some orange or apple slices to make your punch especially pretty.

* If fairy apple juice, fairy cranberry juice, and fairy ginger ale are not available, a grown-up can buy these ingredients at your local grocery store.

Read on for a
sneak peek of…

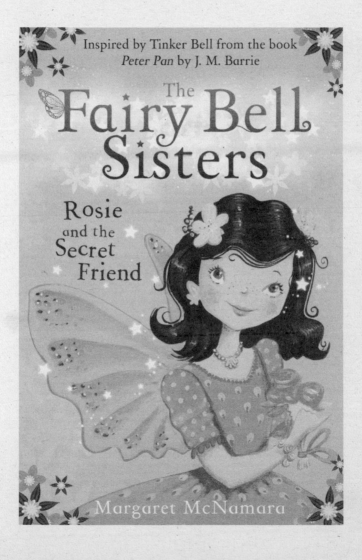

Inspired by Tinker Bell from the book
Peter Pan by J. M. Barrie

The
Fairy Bell
Sisters

Rosie
and the
Secret
Friend

Margaret McNamara

 # Chapter One

All the fairies in the Wide World love
summer – except the Fairy Bell sisters
and their friends on Sheepskerry Island.
Sheepskerry is a fairies' paradise in
autumn and winter and spring, and
summer should be the best season of all.
And for a while, it is.

In June, fairies start doing the things
they've been meaning to do all the rest
of the year: the Stitch sisters sew costumes

for dress-up games;
the Cobwebs
crochet delicate
fairy shawls; the
Flower sisters
take out their
watercolours and
paint under the pale-blue sky.

In July, it's time to throw off fairy
wings and jump in Lupine Pond and
splash in the cool water. Then there
are berries for the picking, all over
the island – pinkberries first and most
delicate; then raspberries, blueberries,
mulberries, boysenberries and finally
blackberries when the days are hottest.
The Bakewell sisters make pies and

muffins with the freshest of the pick, and
the older Jellicoe sisters swiftly store up
jams and jellies for the winter months if
the berry bushes are especially bountiful.

At the end of the day, the fireflies light
up and the summer sun goes down;
the fairies are ready to lay their heads
on thistledown pillows and dream fairy
dreams. But first they watch the sunset
on West Shore, which every night paints
the sky lavender, purple, gold and
scarlet, and needs no fairy magic to be
beautiful.

Summer on Sheepskerry Island would
be perfect, except for the month of
August. In August, the Summer People
come.

Summer People are just that. They're people. Human beings. Mothers and fathers. Girls and boys. Most of them mean well, of course, but still they are immense, bumbling creatures who trample fairy gardens and unleash barking dogs and circle the island in stinky boats and altogether make a fairy paradise into a dreadful place. So fairies stay in their houses under the Cathedral Pines and only come out safely at night.

The Fairy Bell sisters love the summer weather and the fruits and flowers of the garden, but they don't love hiding from the Summer People. Yet hide they must.

To be continued…